Shimmy, Shimmy, Shake!
Let's Bake a Cake!

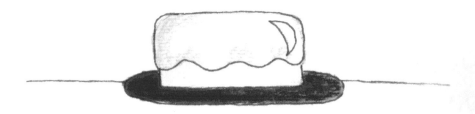

Written by Elizabeth Witcik
Illustrated by Adriana Hayes

Published by Orange Hat Publishing 2011

ISBN 978-1-937165-02-4

Copyrighted © 2011 by Elizabeth Witcik
All Rights Reserved

Printed in the United States of America

www.orangehatpublishing.com

To my husband,
Thank you for always supporting me.
To my children,
Thank you for all of the laughs.
-Elizabeth

To my mom, Gail, who created so many
fun memories in the kitchen.
And to my daughter, Promise, who I get to
create new memories with.
-Adriana

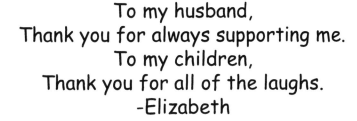

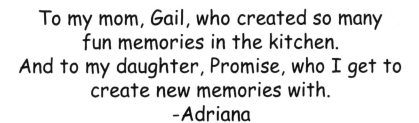

I sit and watch the raindrops slide down the window.

Mom dances into the kitchen and shouts,
"Shimmy, shimmy, shake! Let's bake a cake!"
"Yeah! Let's do it!" I shout.

After washing our hands, I find a bowl, and Mom gets the ingredients. Mom measures the sugar and pours it into the bowl. We each crack open the eggs.

Mom gets the hand mixer and shouts,
"Shimmy, shimmy, shake! Let's mix the cake!"

I measure the baking powder and flour and add them to the bowl.
Flour dust puffs up and I laugh when it hits my face.

Mom thinks she needs some flour on her face too.

I carefully measure the milk, oil, vanilla, and salt
and pour them into the bowl.

Mom turns on the hand mixer and shouts,
"Shimmy, shimmy, shake! Let's mix the cake!"

We slowly pour the batter into the pan.

Mom opens the oven door and shouts,
"Shimmy, shimmy, shake! In goes the cake!"

We set the timer so we know when the cake is done.
Mom shouts, "Shimmy, shimmy, shake! Let's wait for the cake!"

While we wait, Mom and I wash the dishes.

We read books. We draw pictures.

We watch the rain fall outside. Finally, the timer beeps.

I run into the kitchen and shout,
"Shimmy, shimmy, shake! Let's take out the cake!"

Mom carries the hot cake to the cooling rack. While the cake is cooling, we make the frosting.

After washing our hands, I find another bowl,
and Mom gets the ingredients.

I measure the butter, powdered sugar, milk, and vanilla and add
them to the bowl. Mom mixes the frosting,
and then we wait for the cake to cool.

While we wait, we read more books. We color more pictures.

We look out the window and see that it is still raining.
Finally, the cake is cool.

Mom hands me a rubber spatula and shouts,
"Shimmy, shimmy, shake! Let's frost the cake!"

The cake is done. It looks delicious.
"Now what should we do?" I ask.

Mom and I smile at each other and shout,
"Shimmy, shimmy, shake! Let's eat the cake!"
YUM!

Vanilla Cake

-1 3/4 cups sugar

-4 eggs

-2 1/4 cups flour

-2 1/4 teaspoons baking powder

-1 cup whole milk

-1 cup vegetable oil

-1 1/2 teaspoons vanilla

-1 teaspoon salt

Preheat oven to 350 degrees. Lightly grease bottom and sides of two 9-inch round pans or a 9x13-inch pan and then dust with flour.

In a large bowl, beat sugar and eggs with an electric mixer until slightly thickened. Add flour, baking powder, milk, oil, vanilla, and salt and beat until batter is smooth. Do not overbeat. Pour batter into greased pan(s).

Bake for 28-32 minutes for two 9-inch round pans or 35-40 minutes for a 9x13-inch pan. Let cake cool completely before frosting.

Vanilla Frosting

-6 tablespoons butter, softened

-3 1/2 cups powdered sugar

-1/3 cup milk

-1 1/4 teaspoons vanilla

Mix butter and powdered sugar in a bowl. Add milk and vanilla and mix until smooth. 1-2 tablespoons of milk may be added to reach ideal spreading consistency. If desired, add a few drops of food coloring to tint frosting.

CPSIA information can be obtained
at www.ICGtesting.com
Printed in the USA
264954LV00002B